The Naughty Hitchhiker

The Naughty Hitchhiker

A SHORT SPANKING ROMANCE

ANNIKA STOUT

Annika Stout
ORCA - Calle Gil-Vernet 54/55
Les Tapies 1 #1087
Hospitalet de l'Infant, Tarragona 43890
Spain
https://annikastout.com

To Everyone

Please remember:
There are safer ways to get yourself a spanking than
hitchhiking!

Contents

TARA

Just as Tara was about to finish her make-up, one of the bristles of the mascara brush poked her in the eye and she blinked. The result was a black, fine dotted line below her eye as well as on her eyelid.

"Shiiit," she swore, mad at herself for being so last minute *again*.

Quickly, she ripped off a square of toilet paper and applied some cream to dab away the smudged mascara. Her eyelashes stuck awkwardly together which also needed some fixing.

While she was so concentrated that she didn't dare to breathe, her heart was racing.

She had to leave on time. It was the most important day of her entire life. The day she'd been dreaming of. The opportunity she'd been working so hard for.

The *second* interview for her dream job.

Editor.

Not assistant editor. A real editor. At a real publishing house.

Tara Davis, Editor.

She could already see the sign on her office door. Silver and shiny with her name in capital letters.

She rocked the first interview and she knew that this interview was the one where they would pick between her and another candidate. Therefore everything had to be perfect. Her hair, her clothes, *and* her eyelashes.

Just a hint of make-up because too much would look like she was trying too hard. She had to look serious yet hot, because after all there were mostly men in the management team making the decision who'd get hired.

Tara had combined a traditional white blouse with a classic dark blue pleated skirt that reached just below her knees. It was a perfectly professional and proper look, yet anyone who had fantasies like she did would only think of one thing: Spanking.

The skirt was high up in her small waist and therefore emphasized her beautiful round butt.

Tara checked herself one more time in the mirror and tucked a dark blond curl back in its spot. A quick look at the clock on the wall of the living room confirmed she was ok on time. Ok. Not good.

Luckily she wouldn't have to look for parking, there was a garage right below the building of the publishing house.

The dark blue ballerinas looked a bit dusty so she gave them a quick wipe with a paper towel and some olive oil. Perfect.

Purse. Car keys. House keys. And off.

PING!

Tara shuddered at the sound as she turned on her car.

"Holy. Shit."

She had totally forgotten about the gas situation. It's been three days since she took the car last time. And the last time she did, she was in a rush.

What was I late for?

She couldn't even remember why but it was too late to fill up the car that day. The problem was that the gas tank needle already pointed to somewhere in the scary below E area and the closest gas station was in the opposite direction.

Tara checked the time.

No, she thought.

Too late. She wouldn't make it in time for the interview if she drove in the wrong direction.

The bus wasn't an option either. It only left once

per hour and then did the milk run, stopping at every village on the way.

It's okay Tara, she calmed herself down. The needle on the E was only a warning to fill up soon. For safety reasons, there was still a lot of gas left in the tank. Enough to make it into the city. Then after the interview, she could fill up. She even knew a gas station right around the corner of the publishing house.

Tara started driving. Worrying about her empty gas tank had the advantage that it distracted her from her anxiety about the interview.

With one eye on the road and one eye on the gas tank needle, she stuck to the speed limit of the country road, avoiding any unnecessary braking or acceleration.

This will be the longest 30-minute drive of my life, she thought.

Suddenly the car shut off.

It just shut off. No more sound from the motor. Nothing. As if she had pulled the key out of the ignition.

The brake pedal felt heavy. She had a hard time pushing down on it. And as if that wasn't bad enough, the steering wheel was stuck.

Tara used all her strength with both hands to turn it a little bit to the right.

I promise I'll never be late again, she thought, her eyes wide open and pushing down on the brake as hard as she could.

The knuckles of her fingers turned white from the tight grip around the steering wheel but it did the trick. The car slowed down until it finally came to a stop at the side of the road.

Tara opened the door and jumped out of the driver's seat. Her leg was painfully cramping up from pushing down so hard on the brake pedal. Standing up and stretching out her leg quickly stopped the cramp.

Her heart was racing, the adrenaline rushing through her body. With the fresh air in her face, reality returned.

The job interview!

She couldn't lose any time. Calling anyone from her family to come and pick her up wasn't an option. Not only would she arrive late for the interview, but she'd also need to listen to the mocking of them for the rest of her life.

No. There was only one option. Doing something she'd never done in her whole life.

How many times had she been told by her parents and teachers and even her older brother to never hitchhike?

But still. What were the chances that at 9:37 AM on a Wednesday, a psycho mass murderer was going to drive by at this very moment? At this time of the day normal people were on the road. People like her, going to job interviews, dentist appointments, or shopping downtown.

It would be fine. And it would be worth the risk.

Tara Davis, Editor.

Before overthinking things, Tara lifted her arm at the next car driving by.

And the car stopped.

She ignored her racing heartbeat, pulled her hands into fists, and walked right up to the passenger side window of the stopped car. She was ready to fight if necessary.

But the guy inside the car didn't look like a mass murderer. Nor was he trying to attack her. He looked handsome, well-dressed, and somehow familiar.

"Tara is that you?" he asked.

"Jeremy?"

This is impossible, she thought.

She couldn't believe her eyes. Jeremy was her high school crush, the guy who never even bothered looking at her or talking to her. The guy who rolled his eyes whenever she showed up.

Jeremy used to be her brother's best friend. He

and Jack both agreed that she was an annoying little sister.

Tara quickly calculated the years in her head. If she was 32 now, then he should be 36. Eighteen years had passed since she fell for him. A one-sided crush, causing her lots of heartache. Especially when he received a fancy stipend and moved abroad to study engineering.

She smiled at the memory. How innocent she was at that age. And how dramatic, listening to the same sad song on repeat, while feeling sorry for herself.

"What are you doing?" he asked, sounding annoyed.

It was like a déjà-vu. Even eighteen years later he thought she was annoying.

She pointed at the car behind her.

"My car broke down."

"I can see that. What I can't see is your reflective safety vest?"

Tara looked down at herself and back at Jeremy.

Wow. He was cute back then but he had grown into an actual man. He had that type of body that made you feel petite despite your generous curves.

"Yes, ehm-. The safety vest. That's because the brake pedal was stuck and I had to push it really hard and then I got a cramp in my leg, so as soon as the car stopped, I jumped out and-"

"You just jumped out of the car? Did you even check your blindspot to see if someone was coming?"

Tara didn't have a good answer to that one. At least the one she had was surely not what Jeremy wanted to hear. So she just looked at him, at his stunning dark eyes, framed by the black horn-rimmed glasses, and shrugged her shoulders.

"Get in the car," he ordered.

"Just a second," she replied, giving him what she hoped was a sexy smile.

Tara went back to her car, turned on the hazard lights, and grabbed her purse.

Sitting down in Jeremy's car felt strange. There was tension. Lots of it.

She decided to ignore it and just be her happy self. Maybe he thought she was still the annoying teenager but instead, she was an experienced and confident woman in her thirties with a successful career. Especially if today's job interview would work in her favor.

"So not to be rude or anything but there's this important job interview I need to get to. I would be forever thankful if you could just drop me off at the Hampstead Tower."

It was hard to tell if her message had gotten through to Jeremy because he continued driving without acknowledging it. He looked concentrated and serious. His fingers that wrapped around the steering wheel were long, smooth, and taken care of.

Perfectly trimmed fingernails. There was no hair out of place. His crisp white shirt was perfectly ironed. Wrinkle-free perfection.

"Aren't you going to call a tow truck to take your car to a garage?" he asked.

Shit. She didn't want him to know the truth but lying to him? She was a horrible liar and lying to a hot guy doing her a huge favor seemed downright wrong.

"I-. It's -. It's not necessary. I'll be back later. With-. With some gas," she said.

"You ran out of gas?" Jeremy raised his voice, giving her a shocked side glance. "Is your gas tank level indicator broken?"

"No," she admitted.

"Are you kidding? You took the car, despite knowing that you could possibly run out of gas any minute?"

He gave her another judgy look from the side.

Concentrate on the road, she thought, but not because she was worried about an accident. Just because he made her feel so nervous and she didn't want him to see how she was blushing.

"Yes," she admitted, looking out of her window. "But I had no other choice, the interview-"

"There is always another choice. A better choice that doesn't put your life in danger. Do you know how dangerous it is when your car stalls while you're driving? And that's despite the damage it does to your car. Is it really worth all that?"

"I thought I could make it," she said.

"But you didn't. And instead of calling someone to help you or calling a taxi, you decide to hitch a ride? Hitchhiking? Has no one ever explained to you how dangerous it is to get into the car with a stranger?"

His voice was getting louder and louder telling her off.

Tara tried to not stare at him. She felt strangely attracted to Jeremy lecturing her.

His face was so serious and strict. She couldn't help but think of him pulling out his leather belt and telling her to bend over. While her thoughts were going wild, Jeremy went on and on and on, making her pussy throb with excitement.

"Tara!" he raised his voice even more.

"Yes?" she answered, her daydreaming interrupted.

"Are you even listening?"

"Yes, of course. I know it was stupid, I just really felt like there was no other choice."

Jeremy took a deep breath and then stared at the road in front of him, ignoring her again.

"So-? Since when are you back in the country?"

The hot guy in the driver's seat didn't bother answering.

Great. Just great, she thought, feeling annoyed.

First, he told her off and now he gave her the silent treatment? That's not at all how she'd imagined meeting her first true love again after all these years.

At least the lecturing was sexy, his voice sounded so dark and powerful. But the silent treatment? That sucked. If only he could skip those two and go straight to spanking her.

And she really wanted to know if he was back for good or maybe just visiting.

The silence lasted all the way to the Hampstead Tower. Jeremy pulled over, switching on the hazard lights.

"Thank you so much for helpi-"

"After your interview, you will take the bus back home. I don't care if you wait one, two or three hours for it. And this afternoon at 5:30 PM you come to see me and I will take you back to your car to get it started up again. Don't you dare go on your own, putting yourself in even more danger. 34B Kensington and don't be late, I don't have all day."

Jeremy's bossyness, telling her to come see him in the afternoon was the cherry on the cake.

And what happens if I'm late? she wondered.

But she had no time to dwell in her fantasy world. She needed to get to her interview ASAP.

"Thank you again Jeremy. You really are a lifesaver! I'll see you this afternoon."

I'm totally fucked, Jeremy thought.

He'd been successfully avoiding Tara ever since moving back to town and he'd planned on leaving things that way. But she didn't give him a choice. It's not like he could have left her at the side of the road, getting into the car with a fucking stranger.

What was she even thinking, hitchhiking like that? On top of it, wearing such a sexy skirt!

He'd remembered that she was beautiful. Beautiful, funny, and smart.

That's why he left.

He couldn't stand being around her constantly, not able to touch her. The stipend to study abroad was the perfect opportunity to get her out of his head. To forget her. Forever.

But now?

He felt like he'd never been gone. The only difference was that Tara had grown from a teenager into a woman. She did have curves when he left but that didn't compare to the gorgeous body she had grown into. Fuck! She was the definition of a wet dream.

Tara looked so damn sexy in that proper office outfit. The tucked-in white blouse with the pleated skirt was 100% professional. But to someone who had a dirty mind, just like him, the outfit carried another message.

Lift that skirt, bend her over the desk, spank her, and fuck her.

Jeremy tried to concentrate on the traffic, pushing the images of Tara aside that kept on popping up in his head.

In a couple of hours, he'd see her again. He could have avoided it.

No. He should have avoided it.

But somehow the words just slipped out of his mouth. Instead of telling her to call her brother or someone else to help her out, he invited her over to his house. He invited her back into his car.

Why? Why would you do such a dumb thing?

His brain had shut off completely, probably because all the blood rushed down to his cock. His cock that neither cared about friendship nor promises.

Chapter Four

TARA

The interview was a success. The adrenaline of her car running out of gas, fueled by the tension between Jeremy and her on the drive there, made sure she was 100% on fire to show off why she was the best candidate for the position. She knew that if she didn't get picked, there was nothing she could have done better today.

Luckily the wait for the bus wasn't even an hour, giving her enough time to stop by the supermarket on her way home and buy some baking ingredients.

There was no better way to win over someone's heart than by cooking something delicious. Cooking wasn't an option so baking seemed like the perfect alternative.

Tara stood in front of the semi-attached townhouse on 34B Kensington with a tray full of homemade lemon muffins in hand. They were fluffy, still a little warm, and melted like butter on your tongue. The perfect mix of sweet and sour with lemon juice glazing on top.

She'd been so excited to see Jeremy again, that she'd been perfectly on time for once. But who wanted to be on time after being warned to not be late? He was just way too attractive when he was mad. So here she was, an intentional five full minutes late.

OMG!

Her serious outfit from the morning had been replaced by a white shirt tucked into a yellow high rise skirt. This skirt hardly touched her knees, showing off her tanned legs. Maybe not the best outfit to fix a car but certainly a good one to seduce someone.

Jeremy may think she was still the annoying little sister but now she was a fully grown 32-year-old woman. A woman with experience, who knew what she liked and didn't like. And she definitely still liked *him*. A lot.

Eighteen years ago Jeremy was cute but now he was a man. Wide shoulders. Muscular. With real facial hair. And those hands-. He looked like a Greek god.

. . .

Tara took a deep breath and touched the doorbell. Her heart was racing. Hopefully, Jeremy hadn't developed an intolerance to gluten or lactose, then all the baking to win over his heart would have been for nothing.

A dark-haired woman in her thirties opened the door and Tara's heart sank.

Of course, he's already taken, she thought disappointed. Why else would he live in a townhouse? Their two perfect kids and a golden retriever were probably playing in the backyard.

Thanks to her natural acting skills, the smile on her face didn't drop one second.

"Hi, I'm Tara. It's so nice to meet you. I brought over some muffins to thank your husband for his help today."

"Husband? Jeremy? That boring nerd? No, no, no, I've got much better taste than that. I'm just the roommate here and I'm on my way out."

The dark-haired girl grabbed a muffin off the tray and bit into it. With her mouth still full, she mumbled, "Oh my gosh, these are delicious! Can I take another one?"

Tara liked her instantly. Her grinning was 100% real now, holding the tray up.

"Of course, enjoy!"

"I'm Melanie by the way. It was nice meeting you, Tara."

And then Melanie walked away with a muffin in each hand, leaving her alone in front of the open door.

Tara walked inside and closed the door behind her. She followed the hallway which led directly to a big kitchen. This room seemed to be the heart of the house. It wasn't just a kitchen, there was a cozy corner bench, two chairs, and a round table.

"Jeremy?" she called.

"You're late," his dark voice answered right behind her.

Tara turned around. She hadn't heard him coming and didn't realize that the kitchen had two access doors.

"I brought some lemon muffins," she offered, smiling at him.

"That doesn't excuse you for being late. I asked you to be on time. Do you remember what happened last time you were late for something? You put yourself in a very dangerous situation. If you would have left the house a little sooner, you could have filled up the car before and not stop some stranger on the road to hitchhike-"

"Okaaaay, here we go again. Another lecture."

Tara dramatically rolled her eyes, fully intending to provoke Jeremy.

"Well, it's not like I could spank you instead, even though you'd definitely deserve it."

Tara blushed, feeling caught.

Does he know my dirty fantasies? she wondered. He couldn't possibly.

But Jeremy bringing up the topic was the perfect opportunity, she couldn't just miss out on.

"And why is that?" she asked innocently, putting the tray down on the kitchen counter.

"You know exactly why you deserve it."

Fuck, he looks so hot when he gets annoyed.

"Oh yes *that* I know, you've given me a whole list of reasons today but my question was-. Why can't you spank me? Are you too *scared* to-"

Chapter Five

TARA

Tara never finished her sentence. She squeaked in surprise as Jeremy wrapped his arm around her waist, holding her in a tight grip that almost lifted her off her feet with her back being pushed forward by his elbow.

His hand came down fast-paced. Tara was quite impressed by his powerful and confident smacks but Jeremy stopped way too quickly. It had been six, maybe seven smacks, not more. Her skirt and under-wear had cushioned the impact.

The arousing tingling she felt was amazing but it wasn't enough. It was exactly like having a whole bar of chocolate in front of you and only being allowed to eat a tiny piece of it.

Tara laughed. It just came out.

The arousal, the excitement of being in a room with the man she'd always wanted. The embarrassment of facing him now after just getting spanked by him. She felt shy and uncomfortable yet brave and determined at the same time.

Determined to go for it. To ask for it. To push for more.

"You think this is funny?" Jeremy asked. His voice was threatening and oh-so sexy.

Tara wondered if his chest was visibly rising and falling because he was as excited and aroused as she was or if he was simply out of breath from spanking her.

"Sorry, but if that's what you call a spanking, then *yes* it is kind of funny."

Tara looked straight into his eyes, chin up high, her hands on her hips.

Jeremy stared at her. His piercing gaze made her hold her breath and blush at the same time.

Did she go too far?

The words had just slipped out and it was too late to take them back. It was as if time stood still. The tension between them was so thick, you could cut it with a knife. Even though Tara didn't move, her heart threatened to skip out of her chest and she felt the butterflies all the way down between her legs.

What are you going to do now? she wondered, anxiously waiting for Jeremy to make a move.

To spank her. To kiss her. To fuck her.

Anything would do. She just wanted him to touch her and be rough with her.

Jeremy moved a step towards her. He was dangerously close, glaring down at her. Tara had to tilt her head up to be able to hold his gaze.

"Turn," he growled at her, "around."

Tara turned around slowly. She felt Jeremy's breath on her neck.

"Lift your skirt up."

Fuck yes, she thought, biting her lip.

She grabbed both sides of her skirt and lifted them up exposing her naked legs and revealing her white high-rise thong.

Feeling his eyes on her gave her instant goosebumps. Hopefully, he liked what he saw. Her butt and legs were curvy and thick.

"Now go and bend over the kitchen table," he said.

His voice was calm and controlled.

Tara walked the four steps to the wooden kitchen table and bent over as told. As soon as she was in position, she could hear Jeremy approach behind her.

This is it, she thought. She couldn't believe that her fantasies were about to turn into reality. And best of all, it was Jeremy who was about to spank her.

She felt nervous but happy and excited at the same time.

When Jeremy grabbed her thong and pulled up on it, she automatically rose to her tippy toes. The smooth fabric pushed against her pussy.

"You want me to give you the spanking you

deserve? No problem," he said and then smacked down on her bottom.

It was skin on skin, and the whacks came down hard and steady. Again and again and again.

Jeremy lifted his arm high and then pulled through without mercy. He took his sweet time granting every inch of Tara's bottom the attention he considered suitable.

Tara held on to the table, her arms spread out. Every smack of his hand resulted in a grunt from her but mostly she just held her breath. Taking it all in. The spanking. The sensations. His dominance.

As painful as it was, it was the most arousing thing ever. The impact of Jeremy's hand made her butt cheeks shake and vibrate and those vibrations traveled through her whole body. His tight grip on her underwear indirectly rubbed her pussy with every smack.

"Don't move," Jeremy said, letting go of her suddenly.

Tara stayed in position, catching her breath but she was too curious to keep her eyes on the table. When she turned her head, she was surprised to see Jeremy pull out a wooden spatula from the brown terracotta kitchen utensil pot next to the stove. Quickly she turned her head back but it was too late. He'd caught her peeking.

"I've told you not to move."

She could hear him walking back to her now.

"Pull down your underwear!"

What?

Tara froze. Somehow she didn't feel as brave anymore. Would he have asked her the same thing if she hadn't taken a peek over her shoulder? The thought of him seeing everything, *everything,* was embarrassing but crazy titilating at the same time. She couldn't, could she?

Before Tara could overthink things, Jeremy took matters into his own hands. He pulled down her thong in one quick motion and she didn't stop him. The cool draft of air on her exposed pussy felt so good yet so naughty.

Then he rested his warm hand on her lower back. It was the first time ever that he touched her this way. Gentle and protective. She felt safe with him, she trusted him and his touch was the most comforting feeling in the universe.

She wanted more of it. *Needed* more of it. She wanted him to touch her everywhere.

The pressure of his hand on her back increased slightly the second the spatula hit her bottom. A nonvoluntary moan escaped Tara before she held her breath again, clenching her teeth together.

Smack! Smack! Smack! Smack!

The sound was repetitive but Jeremy never hit the same spot twice. He moved up and down, paying equal attention to the left and right side.

Smack! Smack! Smack! Smack!

Tara moved from side to side, huffing and puffing. With every slap of the wooden spatula, standing still got more and more impossible. Her body automatically straightened up when the spatula hit low but Jeremy pushed her back down over the table.

"I said. Don't. Move."

Easier said than done, she thought.

She took a deep breath, only to forcefully blow out the air when the next round of spanking began.

Smack! Smack! Smack! Smack!

The intensity of the slaps increased even more. So much so that Tara couldn't stay put anymore. His hand pushed down hard on her back to hold her in place but that didn't stop her legs from lifting up, stretching out, and kicking.

Her bottom burned like fire.

She'd had enough but Jeremy obviously didn't agree with her. Tara tried counting in her head to distract herself but it was impossible. A smack on her thigh made her hand fly back to protect herself. For a second she rubbed her sore skin before Jeremy grabbed her hand, locking it into the small of her back.

Despite the soreness, a wave of arousal shook her body and made her pussy contract.

Whack. Whack. Whack. Whack.

Tara clung on to Jeremy's hand.

I should not have provoked him this much, she thought.

"I'm sorry," she cried out.

Smack! Smack! Smack! Smack!

"Sorry for what?" he asked, without slowing down.

Smack! Smack! Smack! Smack!

"Hitchhiking. Ow! I'm sorry for hitchhiking."

To Tara's relief, Jeremy stopped.

"That's all you're sorry about? I guess I'll have to continue then."

Smack! Smack! Smack! Smack!

Tara had a hard time catching her breath between the slaps.

"I'm sorry-. For being late-. And for laughing before. Please-. Stop. I've learned my lesson!"

Jeremy instantly stopped, putting the spatula down on the table.

"Let's go get your car," he said and then walked out of the kitchen.

Chapter Six

JEREMY

Holy fucking shit!

What was he even thinking? His brain shut off the moment he saw her in that yellow summer skirt that screamed *fuck me.* And if that wasn't provoking enough, she carried a tray of muffins. A friggin' tray of lemon muffins!

Tara looked exactly like an advertisement from the fifties showing that perfect housewife baking for her husband.

Did she study his secret fantasies somehow?

And to top things off, she literally begged for a spanking. Those first couple of smacks he'd given her hadn't been exactly gentle and yet she'd laughed it off and asked for more.

Fuck, fuck, fuck!

He dreamed his whole life of finding a woman

who was into the same kinky stuff as him. And now? Tara? Really?

Fuck no! He couldn't. He wouldn't.

Jeremy took a deep breath. The look of her picture-perfect pussy surrounded by that glowing round butt was forever burnt into his eyes. He couldn't wait to be alone and jerk off thinking of it. The build-up of pressure in his pants was uncomfortable and begged for an urgent release.

Couldn't he at least have resisted and not pulled down her underwear? But how could he resist when all he'd ever wanted was right in front of him and bent over his kitchen table, moaning away while he spanked her?

Get to your senses man and delete this shit from your memory, it's Jack's little sister!

Chapter Seven

TARA

I t took Tara a moment to push herself back up from the table. For at least two minutes, she just stood there, rubbing her naked burning bottom, and tried to process what had just happened.

Jeremy telling her off, and then spanking her, and wow-. The way he pulled down her underwear had been the hottest thing ever.

Provoking him had gotten her exactly what she'd wanted, even a tad more. Her pussy throbbed, demanding to get touched, but she couldn't. Not now.

She knew she'd better start moving. Jeremy was probably sitting in the car already, waiting impatiently for her.

Reluctantly Tara pulled up her thong. Her fantasies usually didn't stop with the spanking. This should have ended with Jeremy inside of her.

When she noticed the wooden spatula on the table, she couldn't resist. She needed to touch it. The flat piece of wood felt so smooth and soft, it was incredible what a sting it packed.

You'll remember me cooking, she thought with a big smile on her face.

The fact that it stayed behind in this kitchen, reminding Jeremy of her, made her happy.

Jeremy waited in front of the house, holding the front door open for Tara.

Facing him was awkward. Her face was at least as red as her butt as she kept her head down to not fall over her own feet. Her legs still felt a bit wobbly.

Jeremy locked the door and walked to the car but instead of going to the driver's side, he opened the car door for Tara. It was an old-fashioned gesture, surprising but sweet.

"Thank you," she said.

As she sat down she flinched. Sitting down so shortly after the spanking was not comfortable at all.

And then Tara noticed the grin on Jeremy's face. It was the first time she saw him smiling since seeing him again after so many years. His eyes lit up, and all the hard lines in his face vanished. He looked utterly gorgeous.

"You think that's funny?" she snapped at him even though she had to control herself to not grin as well and secretly loved that she made him smile.

"You asked for it, Tara."

And he was right. She did ask for it. And she definitely deserved what she'd gotten.

His voice sounded different now, the anger in it had disappeared and his mood seemed changed.

Is there a tiny chance he enjoyed the spanking as much as I did? she wondered.

The drive to the gas station wasn't long. Neither Tara nor Jeremy talked but the silence wasn't uncomfortable. She enjoyed his presence and glanced at him every now and then, just to make sure that the little smirk still hadn't left his lips.

If only I knew what he's thinking right now.

The seats of his car weren't very cushioned. Leather seats. Fancy but uncomfortable if your butt had just been through a severe paddling with a kitchen utensil. Tara fidgeted in her seat, not able to find a comfortable position.

Jeremy pulled up right in front of the gas station. He turned his head and looked into her eyes.

"Don't. Move," he repeated for the third time today.

Tara nodded, feeling aroused by the secret

meaning of his message. She would not test him this time. Her bottom was not in the condition for any additional spanking. So even though she didn't like that she was stuck in the car now, she stayed in her seat as she was told. Tara watched Jeremy go inside the gas station and pay for two huge gas cans.

"I'll pay you back," she said as soon as Jeremy was back in the car.

"Don't worry about it," he answered.

The drive back to her car was fifteen minutes. She wanted time to stop. To stay in the car with him forever. How could she make sure to see him again after restarting her car? There was so much she wanted to ask him. To tell him.

"Have you been back in town for a long time?" Tara asked.

"I moved back four months ago after being offered a good position. My parents aren't getting any younger and the distance and time change were pretty annoying. Once my ex and I broke up after being together for six years, there was nothing that kept me there any longer."

Six years? Surely the last thing he wanted was another girlfriend now.

Tara felt disappointed. And not just disappointed, she felt jealous. That another woman had had Jeremy to herself for six years. Holding him back from moving back home.

Moving back to her.

"I'm sorry it didn't work out, six years is a long time," she said.

"I'm happy to be back. No need to feel sorry."

Tara watched Jeremy from the side. He looked utterly sexy, how he held on to the steering wheel with those gorgeous hands. The hands that just spanked her. She noticed that he never went above the speed limit, another thing she loved about him to add to the long list of things. Guys trying to show off by speeding were always the biggest turn-off to Tara. She wanted a man who would keep their future kids safe. Tiny little versions of Jeremy in the back seat.

"So, Melanie is just renting a room to you?" Tara asked.

She couldn't help it. She was curious. Melanie didn't seem interested in Jeremy at all but she wanted to be sure that there wasn't more between them.

"*I'm the one* renting a room to Melanie. It's my house, I bought it. But it's big and I don't have time to concentrate on my work, take care of a house, do groceries and cook, so we have an agreement. She is renting a room at a reduced rate and takes care of these things for me."

"Wow! Melanie is your live-in maid?"

"Yeah, kind of."

"Sounds to me like you're spoiled if you can't even clean your own house."

"Spoiled?"

"Yes, spoiled."

"Are you trying to provoke me again?" he asked.

Tara's pussy got instantly wet.

"Maybe?" she dared to say and then quickly looked out of her window so Jeremy wouldn't see her blushing again.

Chapter Eight

TARA

The sight of her car interrupted their conversation. He put on the hazard lights and pulled over behind her car. Then his arm reached across Tara and she held her breath as he touched her legs. It was only a second before he plopped the reflective vest from the compartment of her door onto her lap.

"Put that on," he instructed and then pulled another vest out from the driver's door for himself.

Her heart was racing and melting at the same time. She loved how Jeremy took care of her and made sure she was safe.

"Let's do some CPR on your car," he said.

I wouldn't mind you doing some mouth-to-mouth on me right now, Tara thought while getting out of the car.

They both grabbed one of the heavy gas cans from the trunk and carried them over to her car. Tara unlocked the fuel cap with the key and then Jeremy took over, emptying both gas cans into her tank. His arm muscles tensed up and she couldn't tear her eyes from it. Her mind automatically wandered back to his muscular arms holding her down on his kitchen table spanking her.

Once he was finished she wanted to go to start her car but Jeremy grabbed her arm. His touch was perfect. It was firm but gentle at the same time.

Tara's heart skipped a beat. This was the moment she'd been waiting for most of her life. Finally, she'd get to kiss Jeremy. She turned towards him, quickly moistening her dry lips with her tongue. She was ready for him. Ready for her leg to magically lift off the ground just like in the old movies.

"Give me the car keys," he said, holding his palm open.

Tara tried her best to hide her disappointment and handed over the keys to him. Jeremy pointed to the passenger door. He waited for a car to pass by before getting in.

It was quite entertaining watching Jeremy squeeze himself into the small space of the driver's seat which was adjusted to Tara's size. With ease, he found the handle below the seat and pushed it back. Then Jeremy turned the ignition on but not far enough to start the motor. To Tara's embarrassment, the top hits of her old boy band CD started playing on full blast. She quickly shut off the music.

After a few seconds, he turned the car completely off again and waited.

"This should hopefully get the air out of the fuel lines and will fill up the pressure in the fuel pumps again," he explained.

Tara watched him repeat the same steps as before.

"I knew you studied engineering but I have to admit I'm quite impressed that you know all this," she said.

Jeremy smiled at her. It was that mischievous boy smile that instantly threw her back 20 years

"Don't be, I just looked this up on the internet before. Cross your fingers it works."

Tara laughed.

"Thank you for not making me feel completely stupid."

"You're not stupid at all, don't ever say that again," he said, looking at her.

When their eyes locked, time stood still. Tara wanted to drown in those beautiful brown eyes. As if pulled by an invisible force, their heads moved closer to each other. Tara's lips parted slightly as she angled her head, still holding his gaze.

I love you, Jeremy! I've always loved you.

T he loud ringing and vibrating made both Jeremy and Tara jump in their seats.

Nooooooooooooooooo, she thought and started digging in her bag.

The ringing was even louder once she found and pulled out her phone. The display showed an unknown caller. This could be the call she'd been waiting for. Quickly she opened the door and got out of the car to answer the phone.

"Yes hello?"

"Good afternoon, I would like to speak to Tara Davis please," the woman on the other end said.

"This is she."

"Perfect Tara. I'm Angela, we met this morning at your interview. I'm calling on behalf of Karl van Jonsson."

Tara pressed the phone to her ear, trying to block

out all other noise. She felt the heartbeat all the way up in her throat while holding her breath.

Karl van Jonsson was the chief editor at the publishing house and the one who decided who'd get hired. Her future was in his hands.

"Yes?" she answered.

"Well, I'm happy to be the one to inform you that you've got the position! Congratulations!"

Tara blocked the phone with her hand and started jumping up and down, letting out a very very quiet but very excited long squeak.

"Tara, are you still there?" Angela asked on the other end of the line.

Tara quickly put the phone back to her ear.

"Yes, yes, I am Angela. I just needed a moment to process the information. Thank you so much! I can't wait to start working with you!"

Angela laughed on the other end of the line.

"Wonderful. I'll send the contract over to you by email in a moment so that you can have a look at it. I will also send you possible dates for a meeting with HR to discuss all other details. Just confirm to me what works best for you and I will set it up."

"Perfect, no problem, I will let you know later on today," Tara confirmed.

As soon as Tara hung up the phone she let out a really loud and long scream, jumping up and down again.

Jeremy suddenly stood next to her. She had totally

forgotten about him for a moment. Life couldn't get any better right now. She got her dream job and she was with the man of her dreams.

"You've got the position?" he asked.

"I've got the posiiiiiitiooooooooon," she screamed, giving Jeremy an enthusiastic hug.

Jeremy wrapped his hands around her and lifted her off her feet, spinning her around. When he put her back on the ground he looked down at her, smiling.

"Congratulations! I guess this whole broken-down car thing was worth it after all."

Tara looked up at his sparkling eyes. Meeting his gaze, the butterflies in her belly did somersaults.

"It was," she said. "And not only because I got the job."

Bit by bit Jeremy lowered his head and Tara rose to her tippy toes, staring at his juicy lips. Her heart was hammering inside her chest. She closed her eyes, lifted her chin just a tad more and-

Jeremy pushed her away.

"I'm sorry Tara, I can't."

It was as if she got ripped out of a deep sleep with a fire alarm. One moment everything was perfect and the next her world fell apart.

I knew it, she thought. *Six fucking years!* Of course, he wasn't over his ex-girlfriend yet.

Hiding her disappointment was impossible but

she still tried, putting a cringed smile on her face. Hopefully, she didn't look like *the Joker* right now.

"It's totally fine, I understand," she said.

Taking a step backwards she realized that her car was running again. Jeremy had made it work.

"My car -. Wow-. Jeremy. Thank you so much for everything. I don't know what I would have done without you."

Her eyes turned watery and she quickly turned away from him.

In less than twelve hours she went from not knowing that he was back in the country to being picked up by him, getting spanked by him, landing her dream job, *almost* getting kissed by him to now being abandoned by him. Again.

She knew she was being dramatic when everything turned into a blurry fog in front of her eyes as she walked towards the driver's door. But it wasn't fair. Why bring Jeremy back into her life, just to rip him out of it again and with it a chunk of her heart?

If at least he would have sucked at spanking, but he didn't. He was firm and persistent, delivering a no-nonsense spanking, just as she'd always fantasized about.

She took her sweet time closing the door, waiting for him to call her. To stop her. Change his mind. But eventually, her door shut and she had no other option than to drive off.

Chapter Ten

TARA

Her dream job turned out to be exactly that. It was all she'd ever dreamed of.

Okay, her office wasn't exactly an office but a cubicle in a corner, which was good enough. She did get a triangular metal sign with her name on it, to put on her desk.

Karl van Jonsson was a great boss to have. Young. Funny. Intelligent. A great mentor. He wasn't bad looking either but Tara couldn't change comparing every man she met to Jeremy.

The harder she tried to not think of him the more she did. In her fantasies, in her dreams at night, and in every book she edited, the main character looked just like him.

If it hadn't been for the little bruises on her bottom for a couple of days, she would have thought she'd made him up. Even her friends thought she'd made up the whole story.

"This will be the next great romance bestseller, Tara. You just need to figure out your happily ever after," they'd teased her.

Telling them the full version of the story and showing the proof on her backside was out of the question. It would be the best-kept secret ever between the man of her dreams and herself.

Who knew, maybe in a couple of years when he'd gotten more distance from his ex-girlfriend, he would be ready and contact her. It's all she could hope for at this point.

Tara was convinced there had been something between them. Not something. A lot. She could have hardly imagined all of it.

Why else would he have gotten so mad at her in the car if he didn't care about her at all? And then the kitchen scene. If he wasn't into her and into spanking, would he have actually done what he did the way he did it?

Every other man she'd ever asked for a spanking had given her a heartless tap or smacked on the side of her hip while taking her from behind, thinking that that was what she was talking about. All attempts to get spanked had been disastrous until Jeremy. But he seemed to have known exactly what he was doing. How he had pulled her underwear down when she hesitated. The way he spanked her without hesitating and then even getting the wooden spatula.

No. It was clear. Jeremy was into spanking as well.

Which sucked even more. Finally, a man in real life who was into spanking. Not a random weirdo from the internet, she'd never met before.

Tara realized that even if Jeremy would change his mind, he wouldn't be able to contact her because neither did he have her number nor did he know where she lived.

In a panic, Tara threw all her moral standards and efforts overboard. Years ago she had decided *to not ever* be present on any social media. Now she signed up on all the platforms she could think of, just so it would be easy as pie for Jeremy to contact her, whenever the urge would come up. She kept her profile picture and description low-key and promised herself to delete all these profiles as soon as he would contact her.

———

"Come in," Nick said.

He looked exactly like in the photos that he'd sent her, just not as tall as she'd expected. She couldn't help but compare him to Jeremy. Her gaze dropped to his hands. Could those hands give her what she needed?

I have to give this a chance, she thought.

It's been three months since her car ran out of gas and she still hadn't heard of Jeremy. He continued spooking around in her head but she knew that she needed to forget about him and move on. So she decided to sign up for a dating app, but not just any kind of app. One that lets you find your kinky better half.

Nick's profile was the perfect match. Normal person, with a normal job, and his spanking fantasies and things he wanted to try out pretty much matched hers.

So here she was. Ready to get spanked. Determined to make this work and forget about Jeremy once and for all.

"Would you like something to drink?" Nick asked once they were in his living room.

The place looked nice and tidy. A typical bachelor's apartment with a huge flat-screen TV on the wall. His TV was bigger than if she'd combined four TVs of the one she had. The controller of a gaming console was on the small table in front of the couch.

Did she just interrupt him playing video games? she wondered.

She tried not to judge him but couldn't avoid imagining herself living with a person addicted to video games.

"Just some water, thank you," she said.

Nick came back with two glasses of water and sat down next to her on the sofa.

"So. Here we are," he said.

Tara didn't know what to answer. This was the weirdest date ever.

You came here to get spanked and you're not leaving without getting spanked, she reminded herself.

Surely that would loosen up the tense atmosphere between Nick and her.

"Should we maybe just -?" she asked, making a slapping movement with her hand.

Nick's eyes lit up like the eyes of a kid in a candy store.

"Yes. Of course. I'm totally up for that."

Tara smiled at him and waited but he just looked at her without saying anything. These things were so different in her fantasies with Jeremy. He would simply drag her over his knee and start spanking her.

Jeremy.

Fuck!

This wasn't Jeremy. This was Nick. And it also wasn't one of her fantasies. She knew he had no real experience so far so she had to lower her expectations. With a bit of practice, Nick would surely get the hang of it.

"Do you maybe want me to get over your lap?" she suggested.

"Yeah, that would be cool."

Cool?

Tara took a deep breath and then got over Nick's

lap. She closed her eyes, immediately imagining she was bent over Jeremy's lap.

She felt a tiny twitch in her pussy. Excitement.

There you go Tara, she thought. *You can do this.*

When Nick started spanking her, the excitement died off instantly. She couldn't imagine Jeremy anymore because Nick's hand just didn't feel like his.

It didn't feel right.

He was hesitant, there was no rhythm, and worst of all, Tara felt as if she was cheating. She felt so guilty all of a sudden that she wasn't able to continue.

"Stop Nick, just stop," she said, pushing herself off his lap. "Sorry, but this really doesn't work for me. It's not you, it's me. I'm not ready for this. I have to go."

Nick looked so puzzled when she got up and literally ran away from his apartment. She felt bad for him. After all, he was just trying to find someone to live his kink and be happy with. Just like her. But she wasn't the girl for him.

Chapter Eleven

TARA

Tara wasn't even sad, she was angry. At herself. At Jeremy. At the world.

What Tara needed now was clear.

Chocolate.

Chocolate was the only thing that could help her with this level of frustration. White Chocolate, milk chocolate with whole almonds, and the chocolate with the yogurt filling. Her three favorite kinds. And a jug of milk with it.

After leaving Nick's building, she got into her car and drove to the supermarket which had the parking garage below. She'd be in and out in five minutes and then she'd go home to dwell in self-pity, eat chocolate, and watch TV.

Aisle 11 was the chocolate and cookies aisle. Tara went straight over, not looking at anything else. From there she headed to the fridge to grab the milk. On another occasion, she might have been embarrassed about what the cashier would think of her but not today. She didn't care at all, this was a life-or-death situation.

Armed with chocolate and milk, it was the first time in a while that she felt truly content. She knew what she wanted and she went for it. Now she would enjoy it and have an amazing evening by herself.

She was just about to unlock her car door when someone called her.

"Tara?"

She froze, feeling caught. She heard the wheels of a shopping cart quickly approaching behind her.

"Is that you?"

Tara didn't recognize the female voice. She turned around. It took her a moment to realize who it was. After all, she'd only met her once.

"Melanie?"

Tara was glad that she remembered her name. She was usually horrible with names but she'd liked Melanie instantly and someone who complimented her baking was a friend for life.

"Oh my gosh, I'm so happy I bumped into you," Melanie said. "I can't handle it anymore. Tara this. Tara that. He won't ever shut up! He's driving me nuts with his stupid old stories about you from when you guys were young. Sorry. You're not stupid. He is.

I told him this bro code shit is nuts and he should forget about it. Seriously. Is he thirteen? I don't get men."

Tara stared at Melanie. Her brain had a hard time following the vast amount of information that had just spilled from Jeremy's roommate.

He talks about me? Bro code? What the fuck is the bro code?

"Bro code?" Tara repeated astonished.

"Yes! You know! That stupid bro code shit. Sisters are off limits, under no circumstances can you try to get with your friend's sister, no matter how attractive she is bla bla bla."

"What?" Tara couldn't grasp what Melanie was talking about.

"He talks about me?" she asked, feeling like she missed out on some important detail to make more sense of this.

"Tara! He *does not shut up* about you. *Ever*! And I can't handle it anymore."

Melanie dramatically rolled her eyes and touched her forehead.

"What about his ex?" Tara asked.

Melanie took Tara by the shoulders.

"Tara! His ex is not the problem. Your brother is. He thinks he can't pursue you because they did this stupid bro code pact 100 years ago and he doesn't want to break his promise. And he won't believe me when I tell him it's nonsense. My opinion is worthless because I'm a woman and we *obviously* don't understand the bond between two men."

Tara took a moment to process all the information.

"So just to make sure that I understood this correctly. You're saying he is interested in me but because of my brother and some promise 20 years ago he can't be with me? Because of the *bro code*?"

It felt even more stupid saying it out loud.

"Yes!" Melanie answered. "Exactly!"

Tara looked down at the three huge bars of chocolate and milk in her arms.

"So here I am, buying enough chocolate for a family with four children and getting fat because of a *fucking bro code*?"

Tara dropped her groceries into Melanie's cart. Her anger towards the world and herself had shifted.

"Thank you, Melanie. Please don't tell the police about our conversation. I'm just going to quickly stop by your house to kill someone."

Melanie laughed.

"You go girl! You tell him! I will take my time coming home just in case cleaning up the crime scene takes longer than expected. No need for witnesses."

Tara stopped the car in the driveway and walked straight up to the front door. Her heart was racing as she pressed on the doorbell. She was enraged but the thought of seeing Jeremy made her legs go weak and that made her even angrier.

He didn't deserve her weak legs or her heart speeding up for him. Her confidence took a hit because of him.

Not feeling good enough. Not feeling smart enough. Never being enough for him. Not when she was 14 and not now. Wondering night after night what she had done wrong or could have done differently to change his mind.

Jeremy opened the door, looking gorgeous as usual.

"Tara!?"

Chapter Twelve

JEREMY

How many times had he fantasized about exactly this? About Tara showing up at his doorstep again.

He smiled. He just couldn't hide his excitement to see her. She on the other hand didn't smile. Quite the opposite. If looks could kill he'd be dead by now.

"Would you like to come in?" Jeremy asked.

He stepped back, lifting his arm in an inviting motion. Tara marched inside the house without answering, following him to the living room.

"Would you like something to drink?"

"Let's skip the bullshit, Jeremy," she hissed at him. "Is it true?"

Tara even looked beautiful when she was angry like this. Beautiful and fucking sexy. She'd been feisty as a teenager and she still was feisty now, 20 years later. Taming this fierce woman over his lap was all he'd ever fantasized about.

"Is what true?" he asked.

"The *bro code*?"

Jeremy looked away.

How the fuck does she know about the bro code? he wondered.

He felt caught and stupid. Yes, he knew it was stupid but it just was the way it was. As if the discussions with Melanie hadn't been enough, he'd have to defend his code of conduct once again. Explain it to Tara.

"You don't understand-"

Tara didn't allow him to explain himself.

"I don't understand? Really? Why? Because I'm a woman? You're right, I do not understand why a 36-year-old *adult* man is still holding on to some stupid bro code from his teenage years. This isn't a religious cult. You can make your own decisions and so can I! When were you even in contact with my brother the last time? Why don't you call him right now and ask him if he minds that you spanked his little sister? It's not like you put your stupid bro code first when you pulled down my underwear, did you? Because that, Jeremy, is surely against the bro code. Rule number 273: Don't spank your best friend's sister. Rule number 274: If you do spank her, don't pull down her panties, and definitely do not look at her pussy."

Tara's chest was quickly rising and falling. She

must have run out of words and was instead staring at him.

Jeremy tried to push away those images of her juicy pussy popping up in his head. He needed to stay calm.

"Are you done?" he asked, trying his best to act unaffected by her speech. Hopefully, she wouldn't notice the bulge forming in his pants, giving him away.

She closed her eyes, and dramatically inhaled. He knew she was gasping for more air to continue her speech.

"No. I'm not done. I want my plate back."

Jeremy laughed out loud and Tara glared at him, her eyebrows furrowed.

"Sorry Tara, I don't mean to laugh at you but you're really quite something. Your plate is in the cabinet on top of the sink."

Jeremy sat down on the sofa. Sitting down, his hard cock wanting to come out and play wasn't as noticeable. Besides that, he had no intention of making things easy for her. He didn't want her to leave. He wanted her to stay. Possibly forever.

Tara lifted her chin high and marched into the kitchen. He loved seeing her inside his house. It's as if she belonged there.

He couldn't see her but he could hear her opening the cabinet. Her plate was safely tucked away below a stack of his plates, she'd need to take them all out to get to it.

"Did you find it?" he called.

"Yes," she answered.

"Good. Can you please bring me the wooden spatula from the utensil pot next to the stove?"

The words had just spilled out of his mouth before he could stop it. His cock once again took over the thinking for him. Just like the day that she was in his kitchen for the first time.

"Sorry, what did you say?" she asked.

"You understood right, Tara. The spatula. Now."

There was no backing up now. He wasn't even going to use it. He just wanted to see her expression. Remind her of that day which felt way too long ago. And show her that whether or not she agreed to his *stupid* bro code, he was still the one in charge here.

If you come to my house, you better be ready to get spanked, Jeremy thought.

Plate in one hand and spatula in the other, Tara returned to the living room. She stopped right in front of Jeremy. The look in her eyes was different now. Fiery but also confused. Maybe even aroused. He hoped so.

"Put the plate down," he said, pointing to the small table on the left.

Tara put the plate down as told.

Jeremy looked up at her again, taking all of her in. Even though she was standing and he was sitting, something had shifted. He was in charge again and she knew.

"The bro code might seem stupid to you but it boils down to making a promise and I don't like breaking promises, not even 18 years later. I'm a hundred percent sure though that rules 273 and 274 do not exist, so there's nothing really holding me back right now from taking that spatula out of your hand and repeating what I did to you last time you came over here."

Jeremy spoke calmly and confidently as if he explained something completely normal.

"Give me the spatula," he said, holding his palm open.

His heart was racing, waiting for her to follow his instructions. He knew he was pushing it. Taking a risk.

She stepped forward putting the wooden utensil in Jeremy's hand. For a moment they both held on to it, and even though he didn't touch her, the sudden rush of energy from the connection took his breath away.

Jeremy put the spatula down on the sofa next to him, not paying any further attention to it. He looked Tara in the eyes and gently took her hand in his.

As if he burnt her, she pulled her hand away.

Chapter Thirteen

TARA

She needed to get out of there. To protect her heart from being broken. If there was no future for them, there was no point in staying.

Tara turned, "I have to leave," she said, walking away, not able to look Jeremy in the eyes. Away from his house. Away from him. She wished he would have never stopped for her at the side of the road.

She was almost out of the living room when he caught up to her grabbing her wrist.

"Stop," he said.

Tara twisted around, pulling her arm away from him.

"What do you want, Jeremy?" she hissed.

The hungry look in his eyes intensified even more while Tara was glaring at him, upset that the line between anger and arousal was blurry.

"You. I want you Tara," he said and her legs went weak.

Jeremy came closer and closer. Their bodies touched and Tara could feel his breath tickle her before he cradled her head in his hand and pulled her into a kiss.

The kiss started soft, testing out Tara's response. When she gave up all resistance, kissing Jeremy back, he shifted, wrapping his arm around her back and pressing her against him. His tongue explored her mouth hungry and wanting while his hand wandered down from her back to grab her ass, squeezing it and pushing her against him.

Tara felt the bulge in his pants and rubbed herself on Jeremy. She held onto his arms, his shoulders, and his neck, needing all the support she could get because this man made her legs feel like jelly.

Bit by bit, Jeremy maneuvered Tara back towards the sofa while passionately kissing her and holding her. When the sofa touched her calves, she automatically sat down.

"Ouch," she cried out, pulling the kitchen spatula from underneath herself.

Jeremy was chuckling.

"You better stop laughing because I'm holding the spatula right now," Tara threatened him but was giggling herself.

"We'll see for how long," he answered, sitting down on top of Tara's lap, locking her in place.

She lifted her arms, holding on to the spatula with both hands for dear life. But Jeremy had a better idea. He pulled out her shirt from her jeans and pushed it up further and further, revealing her pointy breasts that were tucked away in a black bra, which he now decided to pull up as well.

She was so determined to hold on to the spatula that she wasn't able to stop Jeremy from undressing her until she found herself tied up with her own shirt and bra over her head. Somehow he had found a way to use the elastic strap of the bra to tie her wrists together.

"And now, I'm going to spank you for driving me absolutely crazy since the day I picked you up at the side of the road," he announced, his eyes sparkling.

Before she could protest, he sat down next to her and pulled her over his lap. Tara still held on to the spatula, her hands tied up. She tried to wriggle off his lap but Jeremy was too strong and quickly put an end to it, wrapping his arm around her waist.

The other hand started spanking her in rapid strokes. The jeans cushioned the impact quite a lot, so it didn't hurt. It was simply bliss, getting what she always wanted from the man she'd always fancied. Jeremy continued for minutes, warming her bottom up gently.

"Lift up," he said, his hands sliding around her waist to open the buttons of her jeans. Tara was eager now to cooperate.

Jeremy was efficient in his task, sliding her underwear down to her ankles at the same time as he pushed down her jeans.

As aroused as she was, this still felt embarrassing but with her hands tied by her shirt and bra and her ankles tied by her jeans and panties now, any protest was useless. She was at Jeremy's mercy and even though she felt shy, there was no other place she'd rather be.

"Your cheeks are nice and rosy already," he said, touching her bottom with his hands. "Now tell me what you want me to do."

What? Was he being serious?

"What do you mean?" she asked, even though she was pretty sure she knew what he meant.

"If you want me to continue spanking you, you'll have to ask me for it," he answered.

As if lying naked and tied up over his lap wasn't already enough, he wanted her to say out loud what she was craving. She'd never told anyone. She knew he knew. He knew this was her thing and she was pretty sure by now that it was his thing too. But asking for it? Then again, she had no other choice, under no circumstances did she want him to stop.

"Please continue spanking me," she said as quickly and quietly as she could.

"Say it louder Tara."

She took a deep breath and repeated, "Please continue spanking me."

"Harder than before?"

"Yes," she admitted.

"Will you let me play with your pussy in between?"

"Yes," Tara answered, blushing with excitement.

His fingers slid along the crevice of her pussy immediately. Tara's moan was a reflex she couldn't hold back.

"I love how wet you are," Jeremy said as he pushed his finger deep inside of her.

Tara moaned an octave higher as he kept on finger fucking her.

"I can't wait to turn your ass the same color as last time. You look so fucking hot with a red butt. I couldn't stop thinking of it since the day you came over."

She remembered that day, when the spatula she held on to now, turned her butt crimson red and sore. It was definitely an unforgettable experience.

Disappointed, she felt his fingers slide out of her. She wouldn't mind him playing with her pussy like that all day long.

Smack. Smack. Smack. Smack.

The smacking was loud, skin on skin. Jeremy took his time. He spanked her slowly, waiting for her reaction before continuing. It was very different from that day in the kitchen. This was an erotic spanking, not a punishment. He made sure her butt was warmed up before increasing the intensity. After every sharp sting of his big hand, he caressed her bottom and his fingers slid between her legs, rubbing her pussy just a bit before lifting his hand again. The line between pleasure and pain became more and more blurry.

The spanking made her butt tremble, sending waves directly to her pussy. Jeremy knew exactly how to smack her. Her pelvis pushed against his muscular thighs, adding to the incredible sensation.

Then he suddenly picked up speed. A quick recession of smacks whacked down on her bottom. Despite the thorough warm-up, the speed of the spanking made her move. She squirmed and wriggled on Jeremy's lap but he held on tightly to her waist, not letting her move much.

Tara got turned on even more by this. Jeremy's strength was so hot and how he kept her in place made her pussy throb with excitement. He continued non-stop for a minute, maybe two.

"Perfect."

He stopped spanking her.

"Your butt should always have this color, it suits you so well. I remember already wanting to do this to you 18 years ago for your silly provoking comments."

Tara giggled, thinking back to those days. She definitely had been a bit of a pain in the butt sometimes, trying to get Jeremy's attention.

A hard slap of his hand stopped her giggles.

Then he flipped her around so that she was lying on her back on the sofa and he was on top of her. His eyes met hers, sending an electric shock through her body. The buttons of his shirt and jeans felt cold on her naked skin.

Kiss me, she thought. And she tilted her chin up.

Jeremy understood. His kiss was rough. He was hungry for her. Starving. And so was she.

The beard stubble scratched her skin but she couldn't care less. All she could think of now was having him close. Being one with him. Connected through their tongues or something else. She felt his erection pushing hard against her thigh. If she'd had her hands free, she'd have already freed his cock out of those tight jeans but her hands were still tied and holding on to the spatula.

"Untie me please," she said.

"Do you promise to not run away?"

"I promise."

TARA

Quickly he removed her clothes from her wrists and ankles to free her. For a moment she rubbed her arms and shoulders that were sore from being stuck in one position for so long. Then she started unbuttoning Jeremy's shirt. She touched his chest, feeling his hot skin and then let her hands glide down over his abdomen to the rim of his jeans. Her thumbs glided over the leather belt. She was distracted for a moment, imagining how his belt would feel on her bottom. The thought caused pulsations between her legs.

She quickly unbuckled the belt and then tried to open his jeans. It wasn't easy as his erection pushed against the jeans, making the buttons very tight. Eventually she managed and freed Jeremy's beautiful dick out of his pants. Again her pussy was throbbing at the sight of his thick swollen cock.

"I want you inside of me *now*."

Jeremy's eyes sparkled and Tara realized she had just said what she was thinking out loud.

"Just a second," he said and got up.

He returned with a box of condoms. When she saw the box had been opened before she felt jealous for a moment.

Why did he have a box of condoms in the house? Who did he have sex with?

"Can you help me with this?" he distracted her from her mind going elsewhere.

Tara took a condom and freed it from the wrapper. She made sure it was the right way around before placing it on the gorgeous almond-shaped tip of Jeremy's cock. She tried to roll it down and managed a bit but she was also scared to hurt him.

Jeremy wrapped his hand firmly around her fingers and helped her pull it down. She loved his hands.

He kissed Tara again, softer this time. Then he pushed her back down onto the big sofa. Tara's heart was pumping in her chest. She spread her legs, making room for Jeremy to get in between her.

His dick nudged against her pussy. Rubbing and teasing. Tara spread her legs wider. She wanted him inside, she just couldn't wait any longer. But Jeremy only let her feel his tip.

Tara felt her wetness, how slippery things were. She tilted her hips to make him slide in but he just wouldn't. Eventually, she moved her arm down to grab Jeremy's cock and take matters into her own hands but Jeremy did not agree.

He pulled her hand away and locked it together with her other hand over her head. Pinned down by Jeremy, she was even hornier, even needier for his cock inside of her.

"I'm in charge Tara," he whispered in her ear before his cock pushed a tiny bit inside of her.

"Do you understand?"

She looked at him.

"I do," she replied.

"Good."

Then he pushed inside of her bit by bit. His width stretched her out, giving her that wonderful feeling of fullness. He went all the way in, their bodies stuck together as close as possible. It was the perfect fit.

After a few gentle thrusts, giving them both time to get used to each other, Jeremy increased the speed. Tara pulled her knees up, giving him perfect access to fuck her hard. His loins and balls were slapping against her with every thrust, causing smacking noises and making everything inside of her vibrate.

He continued fucking her like this until her hands pushed against him, trying to break free from the sheer power of the orgasm approaching. Jeremy didn't let go of her wrists, if anything he pinned her down even harder. His thrusts continued without any interruption, fucking her through the waves of orgasmic bliss, making it last longer than she'd ever experienced before.

When her own waves slowed down, Jeremy's body stiffened up and Tara felt his cock twitching inside of her, expelling his cum.

Finally, he released her wrists and she wrapped her arms around him.

They both started laughing. It was just too much. The emotions, the joy, the perfection of what they'd just done.

For a few minutes, they were just lying there, hugging each other tightly.

"Can I ask you something?" Tara asked.

"Just try and see if you get an answer."

"When did you realize that you're into spanking?"

"I think I was just born that kinky. I can't remember ever not being into it. What about you?"

"Same here," she answered.

"Hmmm. Looks like we're a perfect match then."

"Oh really? So you have decided to forget about that bro code bullshit?"

"No."

"What?"

Tara pushed him away, raging anger flaring up inside of her again immediately.

Jeremy pulled her back into his arms and she let him.

"There's a better solution to this," he explained. "The bro code says: *Sisters are off limits. Unless you plan on marrying her, under no circumstances can you try to get with your friend's sister.*"

"I don't understand," Tara said.

"If I plan on marrying you then it's all good."

"Is this your idea of a romantic marriage proposal?"

"Would you prefer being bent over my knee when I propose? Because I can gladly make that happen."

"Maybe?"

"Mommy, this man is funny."

Tara looked down at her daughter Alicia who was holding both hers and Jeremy's hands to cross the street together.

"Why do you think he's funny?" she asked.

"Just look at him! He gives thumbs-up to every car passing by."

Jeremy and Tara laughed.

"He's trying to make one of the cars stop for him to give him a ride," Jeremy explained. "It's called hitchhiking."

"Hitchhiking?" the little girl asked.

"Yes, hitchhiking," Tara said. "And don't you ever let your father catch you hitchhiking. You'll be in real trouble!"

"It's very dangerous," Jeremy continued. "You

never know who stops for you and if that person has good intentions or not."

Jeremy winked at Tara.

Tara had a big smile on her face, remembering the day she hitchhiked for the first and last time in her life and how she'd ended up with a burning red bottom over Jeremy's kitchen table. Now that kitchen table was their kitchen table and they all lived together at 34B Kensington in the very same townhouse.

"Did you ever do that hitchhiking thing Mommy?" Alicia asked.

"Yes Alicia, I did once. Even I have made bad decisions sometimes," Tara admitted.

"Oh no, did you get into trouble, Mommy?"

Tara and Jeremy exchanged a glance.

"Oh yes, Mommy got into *a lot of trouble* for hitchhiking."

Tara's pussy twitched at the thought of getting spanked. She'd have to ask Jeremy for a spanking tonight. It's been way too long since the last time.

"Oh look, the car stopped Mommy!" Alicia screamed, jumping excitedly.

"Looks like someone will get into trouble tonight," Jeremy said.

And by the look on his face, Tara knew that he wasn't talking about the hitchhiker.

He's perfect, she thought. *My perfect match.*

Jeremy made all her fantasies come true. Her

husband was the most amazing man in the universe. He was her first love and her true love forever.

Thank you for reading "The Naughty Hitchhiker". If you want to stay up to date on all releases of Annika's Spicy Spanking Romances, then head over to **https://annikastout.com** to sign up for her steamy newsletter featuring Mr. & Mrs. Stout's Spanking Blog.

Jack Hunter is the opposite of Olivia. He is the definition of perfection and discipline, working out seven days a week and keeping his apartment spotless.

Olivia's messiness quickly turns into the main source of conflict between the two, causing a tense atmosphere. Her plan to stay out of Jack's life is thrown overboard when he breaks his foot.

Knowing that the accident was her fault, Olivia decides to take care of her grumpy roommate to relieve her guilt. It doesn't take long until sparks are flying and Jack's tough shell starts to crumble.

But when Olivia screws up again, she realizes that she'll never be good enough for Mr. Perfect…

*The Strict Roommate*** is a stand-alone of the Romantically Disciplined Series.

***This book contains graphic love scenes and consensual spankings.*

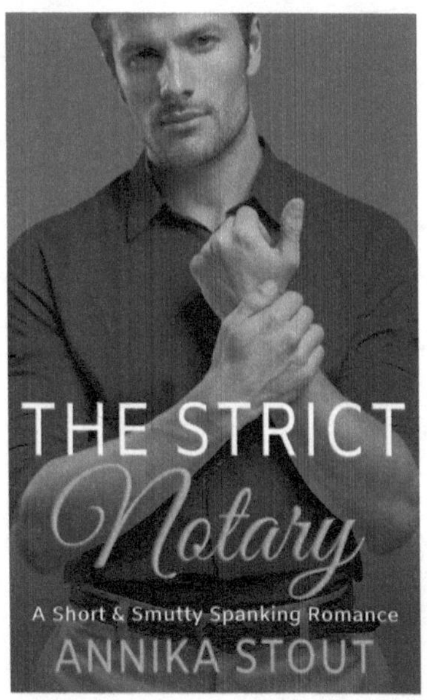

Two-Hours Short Read / Enemies-To-Lovers / Spanking
Level 3 / Spanking Implements: Hand/Cane /Anal Play

"Discipline is if I would take you over my knee right now and give you a sound spanking for kicking a rock at my car and then talking down to me."

Noelia Garrido loves her job as a math and physics teacher but her salary is barely enough to make it to the end of the month.

When she accidentally kicks a rock against a fancy car, her afternoon jog ends abruptly. With no liability insurance to cover the hefty bill, Noelia is desperate.

Rubén Ramírez Armengol is the new notary in town and

the most arrogant person Noelia has ever met. He rejects her suggestion to pay for the car repair in installments and offers her a part-time cleaning job instead.

Working in the notary's office is nerve-wracking but once Noelia realizes that her new boss isn't immune to her charm, she can't stop provoking him on purpose.

When she pushes him a tad too far, Mr. Ramírez decides to teach her his definition of discipline....

This book contains graphic love scenes and consensual spankings.

Two-Hour Short Read / Enemies-To-Lovers / Spanking
Level 3 / Spanking Implements: Hand/Hairbrush /
Anal Play

"The only thing I'll give you is a spanking over my knee if you don't turn around immediately and let me read my book in peace!"

Kimberly Jones loves her new receptionist job, BLT's with extra mayo, and playing soccer. Her days off are spent training on the beach.

When her ball intentionally hits Nicolas Charbonneau, his threat of taking Kimberly over his knee equally shocks and excites her. Little does she know who she's dealing with until the eye candy from the beach shows up at the front desk the next day.

Kimberly will not be the first nor the last employee to lose her job at the hotel if she fails Mr. Charbonneau's customer service inspection.

As sparks are flying, she pushes his limits to find out if he's all empty threats.

Nicolas knows that putting the hotel's reputation on the line by engaging with an employee is a huge mistake. There's only one option....

Hotel Inspection ** is a stand-alone of the Romantically Disciplined Series.

**This book contains graphic love scenes and consensual spankings.*

Two-Hour Short Read / Enemies-To-Lovers / Neighbors-To-Lovers / Spanking Level 4 / Spanking Implements: Hand/Belt/Cane / Anal Play / MfM

*Two-Hours Short Read / Workplace Romance /
Spanking Level 3 / Spanking Implements:
Hand/Ruler/Cane / Anal Play*

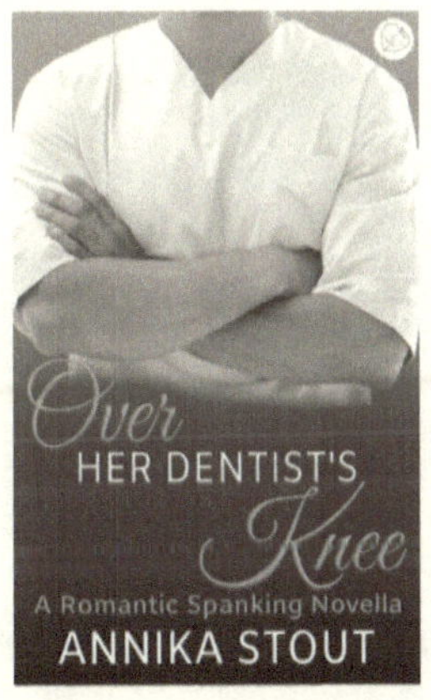

*Two-Hours Short Read / Spanking Level 3 / Spanking
Implements: Hand/Spatula/Cane / Anal Play*

Annika Stout's relationship is a real-life spanking romance. Whenever she's not writing, she is most probably bent over Mr. Stout's knee to find more inspiration.

It wasn't always like that, it took her years to be confident enough to say what she wants and needs. She hopes that her books can help others do the same.

Annika offers contemporary spanking romance without the dark BDSM stuff. Just your typical guy next door, a hot boss or co-worker who isn't afraid to make a strong woman's fantasy come true.

Why not give one of Annika's books to your partner to introduce him/her to your kink? You can read it together or leave a note with it.

If you feel weird about it, just remember that spankos are considered vanillas within the BDSM community.

For more books and updates visit
https://annikastout.com

instagram.com/authorannikastout
tiktok.com/@annikastout_author

9 798227 248695